The BIG Sneeze

Written by
Linda Lamneck Medwig

Illustrations by
Caroline Vlahakis Wissinger

To Isaac,
As you grow I hope
you love to read and enjoy
The Big Sneeze. Follow your
dreams, reach for the sky, the
moon and the stars!
Linda
Lamneck
Medwig
2016

Printed in the United States of America.

ISBN: 978-1-63385-099-6

Library of Congress Control Number: 2015915945

Illustaions by Caroline Vlahakis Wissinger

Designed and published by

Word Association Publishers
205 Fifth Avenue
Tarentum, Pennsylvania 15084

www.wordassociation.com
1.800.827.7903

Dedication

*This book is in Memory of my mother, Caroline Vlahakis Wissinger.
Mom's unconditional love and incredible artistic talents
made it possible for this "dream" storybook to come to fruition.*

*This book is dedicated to my three grandchildren,
Hudson, Roman, and Haylee.
Although you were a twinkle in our eyes when this book was first written,
you now make me smile everyday and keep me young.*

Love, Mimi

Preface

Many years ago, while I was attending West Liberty University in West Virginia and working toward my Bachelor of Arts degree in Elementary Education, I was taking a children's literature course. One of our assignments, while doing my student teaching, was to write a children's book. Thinking about a children's story wouldn't be too difficult, but what about the illustrations? I knew that illustrating the book would be a little more difficult. Our professor told our class that as long as we wrote the story we could choose someone else to illustrate our books. Immediately I thought of my mother, Caroline Wissinger. She was an extraordinary artist! She studied art in college, went on to teach art from preschool through high school, worked as an interior designer and used her artistic talents in many other ways. In her late 60's she had a home based business of making and selling Bandboxes in the style of the 18th century. These were a unique collection of Bandboxes exquisitely reproduced from original antique engravings. Her work was featured in many prominent magazines. My mother was humble and modest about her artistic ability, but was delighted to do the illustrations and bring my story to life.

The Big Sneeze is the story of two bunnies who have a big problem that keeps them apart. But one day something amazing happens that brings them back together again.

When the original story was written, the characters had different names. Now that I'm a grandmother, I thought it would be a wonderful experience for my grandchildren to have their names as part of the story. So we have Romie (for grandson Roman), and Rosie (a name my niece suggested). Children love to hear sing-song names, repetition and alliteration in stories, so both Romie and Rosie have the long "o" sound and names that are easy for children to pronounce. The farmer in the story is Farmer Hudson Haylee after grandson Hudson, and granddaughter Haylee. My daughter Kara told me that Haylee means "hay meadow" so what could be more appropriate for the farmer's last name?

Caroline Vlahakis Wissinger

When the Professor read my story and looked at my mother's illustrations, she immediately said she thought I should have the book published. Now, 40 years later, my dream has come to fruition. Why did it take so long to have this published? Life! Life got in the way, as so many times it does, and we put aside our dreams for work, raising a family, and then taking care of aging and ill parents. My biggest regret is that I did not have *The Big Sneeze* published while my mother was living. About eight years ago, my mother developed Alzheimer's disease, and as her mind began to deteriorate, I could see that she was so sad that her artistic ability was no longer a vibrant part of her being. She passed away November 4, 2012. Because of the devastation of the disease, I have committed and continue to support the Alzheimer's cause. A cure MUST be found! Part of the proceeds from the sale of this book will go to the Pittsburgh Chapter of the Alzheimer's Association in memory of my mother, Caroline Wissinger.

I would like to acknowledge my husband, Terry, my rock to lean on; my two beautiful daughters Rebecca and her husband Rich; and Kara and her husband Dan, who blessed us with three incredible grandchildren. Thank you to my sister Sandy, who is the best and gave me the push that I needed; brother-in-law Bob; nephews and niece Scott, Tyler, Allison, and other family members and friends who make me laugh and encouraged my work. Thank you all for your love and support!

Romie is a happy little roly-poly bunny. Romie loves everyone and naturally everyone loves Romie.

Everyday Romie and his friends would run and play in the fields. Romie has lots of friends, but he has one friend who is very special. Her name is Rosie. Romie and Rosie loved to hear friends call their names because they sounded almost the same. Romie, Rosie! Romie, Rosie!

All day long Romie and Rosie would run through the fields chasing butterflies and birds, and hopping over rocks.

One day Romie saw some beautiful blue cornflowers.

They were so pretty he decided to make Rosie a wreath for around her neck.

Rosie said she loved the wreath and would wear it everyday. Romie said, "Rosie, you are the, - the, -the, -prettiest...

AH- AH- AH- AH-

When Romie stopped sneezing and opened his eyes Rosie was not there.

He sneezed so hard he blew her over a hill!

Everytime Rosie would come near him, he would sneeze and blow her away.

He sneezed and blew her over a rock. He sneezed and blew her over a butterfly bush. He sneezed and blew her over a pond.

Romie became very sad. He couldn't play with Rosie anymore because every time she came near him he would sneeze and blow her further and further away.

Romie missed Rosie. All of Romie's friends felt sorry for him and wanted to help him. "What can we do to help you?" they asked. "When you are sad, we are sad too."

They tried holding his nose but...

that didn't work.

They told him to stand on his head but...

that didn't work.

They told him to cross his ears but...

that didn't work.

All he could think about was how much he missed Rosie. He looked up and there she was. Romie said, "Rosie-

AH- AH- AH- AH-

AH- CHOO!"

And this time he blew her over the barnyard fence into Farmer Hudson Haylee's garden.

Farmer Hudson Haylee chased Rosie under the fence with his big broom. As Rosie was running under the fence she lost the beautiful blue cornflower wreath that Romie had made for her.

She ran back to Romie to tell him how she lost her blue cornflower wreath.

What do you think happened? ROMIE DIDN'T SNEEZE! Rosie was so happy she hopped up and down with joy. Their friends hopped up and down with joy too. Romie said, "Rosie, I think it was the blue cornflower wreath that made me sneeze."

Now Romie and Rosie can run through the fields together again and chase butterflies.

Romie thought the fields never looked as pretty, and the sun never shown as brightly...

... and the world was a beautiful place, as long as Rosie was there too.

Hot Chocolate
BOOKS